THE GOOD ENOUGH AMERICAN NOVEL AND OTHER VERY SHORT STORIES

BY

DONALD CARSON

ISBN 978-1-7373417-0-3 (Paperback Edition)
ISBN 978-1-7373417-1-0 (EPUB Edition)

Library of Congress Control Number 2021911371

Cover and book design by Ebook Launch (www.ebooklaunch.com)

Printed and bound in the United States of America

First printing January 2022

Published by Favorite Trick Books
www.favoritetrickbooks.com

*To Alexandra, who is my best editor,
kindest critic, and favorite person.*
*To the No-namers, who do have names, of
course —*
*Daniel, Jeremy, John, Laurel, Sarah, and
Summer.*
*Your encouragement and advice is a major
reason this book exists. Special thanks to
Laurel for copyediting.*

*To Ali Shaw and Indigo Editing,
for sponsoring the
Mini Sledgehammer Writing Contest, where
several of these stories were originally written.*

*And to my parents, Betsy and Mike, for
pointing me down the word-strewn path
and cheering me on as I traveled it.*

THE GOOD ENOUGH AMERICAN NOVEL

AND OTHER VERY SHORT STORIES

STORIES

I'm Your Author 1

A Good Day for Short People 10

Special Delivery 16

Love in the Time of La La Land 22

Destination: Bingo 28

Daughter of the Circus 38

Do You Know Remy Duvall? 44

A Field of Fresh Snow 49

Contrary Creatures 56

Hearing Things 61

The Other Shoe 67

Autonomy 72

The Heart Wants What It Wants 79

The Good Enough American Novel 91

I'M YOUR AUTHOR

Wanderer woke, groggily, with only enough energy to move his eyelids upwards and allow his surroundings to push into his head through the foggy layer between reality and his brain.

A white ceiling, devoid of any fixtures, stared back at him.

Where was he? And why was his name "Wanderer"? It didn't sound like a proper name at all — more like a card in a fortune-telling deck.

He heard what sounded like a seagull yell, and then another gull yelled back, and he thought he must be by the sea.

But what was he doing here? And then the answer came to him, floating up from the depths of his soul like a dead fish from the ocean floor: he was a professional juggler, and he was here to juggle.

He sighed, disgusted. That wasn't a proper job at all! Butcher, or baker, or management consultant. Those were proper jobs. Juggling was just something you did spontaneously if suddenly handed two very hot meat pies. It wasn't something you could make a living at.

His eyes shifted to the threadbare clothes hanging on the white chair. Judging from the state of them, he wasn't making much of a living.

The door made a knocking sound, and Wanderer groaned. The worst way to start a day was to be tired and confused and have to shelve all those feelings to put on a pleasant face for someone else.

He lay there, hoping the sound wouldn't happen again.

It did.

Groaning again, he heaved himself off the mattress and found that he was marginally dressed in a white cotton adult onesie.

He groaned yet a third time.

If someone had dressed him, fate was cruel. If he had dressed himself, he had very poor taste.

The door continued to make the sound, and he tried his voice. It worked.

"Hold your horses!" he shouted.

The door didn't seem to care. It continued to make the sound.

He pulled on a stained white cotton blouse and patched green denim pantaloons and padded to the door.

Opening it, he looked around. There was no one there.

"Down here," said a shrill voice. He looked down.

A very small woman was standing there. She was about two feet tall.

"Who are you?" Wanderer growled.

"I'm your author," the tiny woman said, marching past him and into the room, where she looked around, hands on hips, nodding as if she were satisfied with something.

"Looks good," she announced. "I did a great job of describing this."

"Now look here…." Wanderer began, but then he felt something give in his throat. He tried to say something more, but his voice had stopped working. He couldn't even move his lips.

"It's time for listening," the small person said. "You'll get plenty of dialogue later, believe me."

Wanderer believed her. But he really wanted his dialogue right then because he had a lot of things to say to this unwelcome guest, and many of them were satisfyingly hostile.

"Here's the deal," the author said. "I've sorta run out of inspiration, so I'm doing an exercise someone in my writing group suggested where I come into the story and see if that doesn't shake something loose. I screwed up, though, which is why I'm so short. I meant to type 12 feet tall, but I left out the 1."

Wanderer wanted to laugh evilly at this, but his face was now completely non-functional.

The woman trotted over to the bed and pulled herself up on it, sitting with her feet dangling off and bouncing up and down meditatively.

"OK, so interrogate the protagonist…." she said to herself. And Wanderer suddenly found his throat unstopped.

"This is outrageous!" he yelled.

The woman had pulled out a miniature pad and looked at him interestedly. "It is? In what way?" She began to write rapidly.

"Well, I mean —" Wanderer was at a loss, since he had no idea what was going on.

"Tell me," the woman said, reaching into her pocket and pulling out a cloth baggie. "Would it help to nibble on a bit of birdseed?"

"I don't want your birdseed!" Wanderer howled. He knew that much, at least. "I want a nice stack of flapjacks!"

"Iiiiiinteresting," the woman said, replacing the birdseed in her pocket and scribbling away. "What else?"

"Are you taking my order?" Wanderer asked incredulously.

The woman didn't look up. "I might be," she said.

"Well in that case," Wanderer said, "I wish bacon to accompany my flapjacks. Much bacon. And I wish butter to be melting upon them. And whipped cream. And —" He paused, and then brilliance struck him. "Fresh sliced peaches. Yes. That's what I want."

The woman looked up. "But what's your motivation?" she asked, cocking her head.

"Hunger?" said Wanderer, wondering if this were a trick question. This tiny person was not to be trifled with.

"Take a look outside," the woman said, and the blinds on the windows, which Wanderer had not noticed before, all retracted at once. He was staring at a fine view. A seacoast, on a stormy day. Clouds were scudding, and roiling, and other things clouds did. Seabirds drifted and dove on the wind.

"How does this make you feel?" the woman asked.

Wanderer searched for the right answer. He did not want to make this little woman who had so much power over him angry. He wanted to make her proud. He plumbed his own depths for something profound. "Like … like there are forces larger than myself?"

The small woman grinned and scribbled mightily in her notebook. "Good, good," she said. "This is good."

She stopped writing and stared at him expectantly.

He stared back. Did she want him to go on making up profound things to say? He was still quite unclear on how he was supposed to be helping her.

Then Wanderer remembered. He was a performer, dammit. A juggler, true, but were there not many things to juggle? Words, for example. Situations.

So juggle this situation, he told himself.

"When I woke up this morning," he said, meeting the gaze of the bright, unsettling little eyes, "for a moment I forgot who I was. Then it came to me: I am Wanderer, juggler extraordinaire!"

The woman was beaming.

"And yet —" Wanderer gestured grandly to the remainder of his outfit, still laid across the back of the chair: a faded felt burgundy cloak and green woolen stockings with conspicuous holes in them. "And yet, I find myself in the most tattered of apparel. The juggling business has been difficult."

He strode to his stockings and pulled them on as he talked, slipping his feet into the scuffed leather boots with the tarnished buckles and throwing the cloak over his shoulders. Then, donning the black felt tricorn hat with the white plume he found on the chair, he puffed out his chest and exhaled.

"Yet I shall make the best of it!" he said.

The small woman clapped. "Bravo!" she yelled.

"Thank you," Wanderer said. Then he bowed, turned and ran for the door, pulling the key from the bedroom side, closing it hastily and locking it on the hallway side with the selfsame key.

He heard an angry squawk from within the room, then the sound of pattering feet and tiny fists pounding on the door at about knee level.

Wanderer smiled. His guess had proven right. Why had this miniature person who claimed to be his author needed him to open the door this morning? Apparently her authority was limited. And if she had created him, with his wretched profession, uncertain garments, and confused thoughts — well, she couldn't be all that good at her job.

Taking the key with him, he trotted down the hall, looking for the front door. The pounding continued behind him.

Wanderer stepped out onto the front porch of the inn and breathed deeply of the sea air. He was free. Now perhaps he could begin to write his own story — or at least be allowed to wander in peace.

But first, flapjacks.

A Good Day for Short People

Doug closed his MacBook and slipped it into his messenger bag. He needed to leave now if he wanted to make the pitch.

He was one of the founders of the boutique advertising agency 4.5 Clowns. In fact, he was the .5. It was the other four partners' way of making fun of him for being short. He'd been a tiny baby who'd grown into a smaller-than-average toddler and finally, in college, achieved his final height of five feet and three-quarters inches.

And now, it seemed, he got all the small clients, as well. He was about to cycle across town and try to convince a family-owned carpet business to use 4.5 Clowns for all their advertising needs.

Nancy, another of the partners, stuck her head in his office as he shouldered the bag and patted himself down to make sure he had his wallet, keys, and other essential cargo of the modern human.

"Off to see the Rug Wizard?" Nancy asked. She stood six feet and laughed easily. Tall people seemed to move through the world with such little effort, even when they wore a Fidel Castro-esque military uniform to work every day and spiked their short gray hair straight up toward the heavens as Nancy did.

"Indeed." Doug looked up at her.

"You can take my car," Nancy said, rattling her Porsche key fob in his face. "You don't have to risk your life on that bike."

"That's very kind," Doug said. "But I like riding."

Nancy shrugged. "Good luck," she called as Doug slipped past and trotted down the hall. "Bring us back some of that juicy rug business!"

Though he was the eldest of the partners, they often treated him like a kid, simply because they were all a foot taller than he was. Or, he often worried, was it only because he was short?

Was there something about him that welcomed victimization? After all, Napoleon was said to have been short. And look what he accomplished.

Considering the size of the crowd protesting near the Rug Wizard headquarters, Doug was glad he was on a bike. He shuddered to think how the masses would have reacted to him trying to nose his way through them in Nancy's red Panamera. He dismounted and threaded his way through the picketers, who seemed to be angry at the way a Chuck E. Cheese employee had mistreated a patron's emotional support animal. IF THIS IS HOW YOU TREAT FERRETS, screamed a sign, HOW DO YOU TREAT PEOPLE??!!

Regular citizens could be so inarticulate. That's why ad agencies existed. Doug paused for a moment, trying to imagine the sign he'd have written. Maybe something like YOU WON'T WEASEL OUT OF THIS ONE, CHUCK! Or, more to the point, A RODENT SHOULD KNOW BETTER.

The Rug Wizard was just around the corner from the Chuck E. Cheese. Doug locked up his bike and went in the front entrance, where the receptionist led him behind the counter and down a hallway.

"Here's Mr. Aydin," she said, ushering him into a small office. The man behind the desk looked up, then stood, beaming, and extended his hand. He and Doug were exactly the same height.

"Another short guy," the man said. "I like you already. Please, call me Ali."

Doug sat down in the chair and was struck by its comfort.

"It is delightful, no?" the other man said. "It's not the size of the office, but the quality of the furnishings. You can say the same about people, maybe."

Doug agreed.

"Before you begin," the man said, "please let me tell you things I may have left out when I talked to your Clown people. I didn't want you to make any special effort for pitching. I've seen your work, I like it. And now I've met you, I like you. But I was perhaps not completely open at first because it is not done deal yet."

Doug leaned forward.

"Rug Wizard is acquiring Carpet King and Flooring Genie all in one swoop!" the man exclaimed. "We'll be largest carpet sales and installation service in the ten-state area! I will be little guy with big empire! And for this, we need big campaign. Very big. And I think you Clown people are the ones to do it."

An hour later Doug pedaled back to the office in a very different mood than he'd been in on the trip over. It wasn't a glamorous account, but the new business he'd just landed was going to bring in enough to put it in the top five in billings, at least. And it was definitely the first time 4.5 Clowns had named and created a new brand from scratch.

As Doug came in the door of his office, whistling a few bars from Hamilton, he caught Nancy sitting on his desk running her hand across the back of the taxidermied rooster his brother-in-law had given him. "So you can make jokes about your cock," Ed had explained. Doug didn't make jokes about his cock because it wasn't workplace-appropriate, but he did bring the stuffed bird into his office because he liked it. So did Nancy, who couldn't resist stroking the feathers even though Doug had asked her repeatedly not to.

"I won't tell you again — STOP TOUCHING IT!" Doug hollered before he thought. Nancy looked unaccustomedly stricken, and Doug felt unaccustomedly fantastic.

"It's OK, Nancy," he said. "I just don't like you putting your hand on my cock without permission." Then he laughed the laugh of a six-footer.

It had been a good day for short people.

SPECIAL DELIVERY

The mail van struggled a bit. Its chains, medi-ocre like the rest of the vehicle, often failed to bite into the compacted snow. Flakes still swirled around the windshield as Goldie pulled off to the side of the road, the van sliding un-easily toward the mailbox, and reached for the next batch of letters.

Opening the window, she deftly operated the mailbox door with her gloved fingers, dropped the letters in and shut the door.

Flake density doubled as Goldie continued on her route. Not exactly a blizzard, but enough snow to slow her down. She'd have to work late tonight and, with the sun setting at four o'clock, a lot of driving in the dark. Luckily the one thing that worked like a champ in the mail van was the heater. It was howling enthusiastically at the moment and putting out enough heat to warm the inside of a stadium.

Goldie's phone buzzed, and she bent forward to tap the screen with her nose to answer it. A little trick she had picked up when she was too cheap to buy gloves that worked on a touchscreen. She always had her earbuds in, so she was all ready for the phone call that inevitably came right around now.

"Ma?" she said.

"Who's this?" quavered the voice on the other end of the line.

"It's me, ma, your loving daughter," Goldie said. "You called me, remember?"

"Oh, yes," the voice said, hesitantly, as if negotiating the sale of something it had no idea the value of.

"How are you doing, ma?" Goldie said, leaning on the big steering wheel to edge her van up to a bank of mailboxes for some McMansion development. She loved these group mailbox situations. Saved a lot of time.

"Well, there's this man at the door who says he knows me," her mother said. "He says he's my lawyer."

"Yes, ma, remember," Goldie said matter-of-factly. "Your lawyer, John Doe, had an appointment with you this afternoon."

"Hmmm," the voice said. "I thought the name seemed suspicious."

"You did right to call me, ma," Goldie said. In fact, the only reason her mother had called her was because she had put a big note by the phone that said IF YOU HAVE QUESTIONS CALL THIS NUMBER. "But that's his real name, and he's really your lawyer. You should let him in. He'll help you with your will."

"What do I need a will for?" her mother asked petulantly. "I'm just fine."

"I know, ma, you're tops," Goldie said. "This is just in case. Hell ma, even I have a will. It's just in case, ma."

"All right then," the voice sighed. The line cut off, just like that. Goldie's mother wasn't one for hellos or goodbyes.

Goldie felt that spreading numbness in her gut that after many years she recognized as sadness. Something about the cold winter days, the snow in the headlights, made her nostalgic. It seemed like just yesterday her mother had driven her to college and insisted upon carrying the heaviest suitcase all the way up the stairs to the middle of her dorm room.

It was with these thoughts swirling around in her head like snowflakes that she reached the end of a cul-de-sac and prepared to spin the big steering wheel around in a U-turn.

But what was this? Something was funny. She checked her GPS to be sure. This road was no longer a cul-de-sac. She shook her head and whistled. That call with her ma had done a number on her brain.

Either that or some eager developer had carved out a street where there never was a street in just one night.

OK, she'd bite.

She eased the mail van down the street that shouldn't be there and then made a sharp in-take of breath. She couldn't help it.

There on the right was her old house, the one she'd lived in as a child. Except it was supposed to be about 1,500 miles from here.

She looked down into her stack of letters and, sure enough, there was a letter addressed to her.

Automatically, she picked up the letter, rolled down the window and delivered it into the box.

Then curiosity got the best of her.

She left the oven-strength warmth of her van and let her boots lead her through the piling snow toward the front door of the house.

Knocked on the door. Realized suddenly she'd been holding her breath and let it out explosively.

The door opened.

"Hello," said a girl who looked powerfully like Goldie had looked at 14. "I've been waiting a long time for this." The little thing looked so hopeful. She was standing on the world's door mat, about to be let in to the rest of her life.

And she was so thin. So damn thin.

"Well, I haven't," Goldie snapped and then realized how futile it was to be rude to her own self. "I'm sorry, girl. It's just that you've got a lot of living to do, and life isn't always how you plan."

"I know," the girl said, fixing Goldie with her own gray eyes. "It's just that all times are now."

"All times are now," Goldie repeated. And then she got it. Her past was telling her to live in the present, to embrace the moment she was in, instead of obsessing over the moments she'd had or might have.

"Thank you, Goldie," she said, leaning down and taking her own cheeks in her hands. Then she kissed herself on the mouth.

"You're welcome, Goldie," the girl said and grinned roguishly before shutting the door.

"All times are now," Goldie murmured as she clumped back through the snow to her mail van. Already the phrase was losing its shine. She was forgetting the immediacy of what it had meant just seconds ago. Life was like that.

But it was good advice nonetheless. Tonight she'd tell her ma all about it.

LOVE IN THE TIME OF LA LA LAND

Author's note, which includes spoilers: La La Land *is a 2016 romantic comedy-drama-musical about the relationship between a jazz musician and an actress who grow apart while pursuing their careers and do not end up together at the conclusion of the film.*

"So what did you think of *La La Land*, Jennifer?" he asked her.

She wrinkled her nose. "I thought it was OK. Maybe not as good as all the hype."

He nodded. This was where he declaimed for the next few minutes upon his favorite topic, Modern Romance.

"It's one of several films I've seen recently wherein the two love interests do not end up together at the end," he said. "This is a disturbing trend in modern cinema."

She nodded, absently, and he knew he'd lost her. This date was not going well.

The bell rang.

"OK," said the shrill little man with the megaphone. "Speed daters, stand up! Move down one table."

"Nice to meet you, Jennifer," Mike said. He stood up, moved to the next table on his right and sat down. The chair was still warm from the heat of one of his rivals' posteriors.

"Hi," said the woman across from him. "I'm Jennifer."

Mike looked puzzled. "But —" he started. "The last woman I spoke with was also named Jennifer."

"It's a common name," the woman said, and he watched the muscles under her eyes compress in annoyance. "Are we going to spend the whole time talking about my name? Are you going to tell me your name toward the end in a big reveal? Or may I know it now?"

"Sorry," Mike said. "I'm Mike."

Now it was the woman's turn to look puzzled. "The last man's name was Mike," she said."

"It's a common name," Mike said. "So can I just ask you right up front — have you seen *La La Land?*"

Five minutes later, Mike was seated in front of a different woman. The last few minutes with the previous Jennifer had not gone well. She had not seen *La La Land*, and after that revelation the dialogue had fizzled a bit.

"Hi," he said. "My name is Mike."

"This is really funny," the woman said. "The last two guys have been named Mike."

"Your name doesn't happen to be Jennifer, does it?" Mike asked.

"It is," she admitted. "But I go by Jennn. With three Ns. I like to fuck with people."

Mike nodded. "Have you seen *La La Land?*" he asked.

"Yeah," she said. "It's one of several movies I've seen in the last while where the love interests don't get together at the end. What did you think of it?"

"I totally agree," Mike said, astonished. Here was a Jennifer he could talk to! "What do you think it means?"

"I think," said Jennn of the Three Ns, "that it is brilliant. I mean, it often happens in real life. For every person you marry, there are hundreds you didn't. And just because you have a story-book romance with someone doesn't mean you end up together."

"Hundreds?" Mike said weakly.

"Not literally," Jennn laughed. "I mean in my case, probably not more than fifty."

Mike swallowed.

The bell rang.

The man with the megaphone told the speed daters to move on.

"Really nice talking with you," he said to Jennn.

"You too," she said. Their eyes locked as he got up and moved to the next table.

Another woman. This time he was not surprised that her name was Jennifer, nor that he was not the first Michael she'd talked to that evening.

As Mike moved down the line of women sitting at tables, every single one of them named Jennifer, he kept glancing back at Jennn. And when he did, he found her looking at him as well.

"What did you think of *La La Land?*" he asked Jenny, who was somehow managing to chew gum and drink wine at the same time.

"I hated it," she smacked. "I didn't know it was going to be a musical. Plus, like, the ending sucked."

Mike nodded, and the little voice in the back of his head that helped him endure these kinds of events said "check, please!"

Finally after two more Jens, a Jenni, and a Jennyfer, it was over, and he had given both his first and second votes to Three-N-Jennn and his third to Jenni, the least objectionable of the rest. He thought that would be enough to land a date with Jennn for the remainder of the evening, but when the votes were tallied, the wheels of fortune spun, and the music stopped, he ended up with someone he hadn't even voted for. Jenny.

"There's lots of great sports bars around here," Jenny said. She was still chomping on her wad of gum. He tried, and failed, to admire her for the vigor with which she chewed it.

Over her shoulder he watched as Jennn moved down the block away from him, on the arm of another Mike. It had begun to rain, and he opened an umbrella over both of them.

She looked over her shoulder and caught his eye then, and smiled, and his heart thudded, and his chest ached, and his mouth dried out as suddenly and thoroughly as if a dentist's suction tube had been inserted into it.

He knew he'd never see her again.

DESTINATION: BINGO

Harold Anderson drove his indoor mobility scooter down the ramp into the garage where his outdoor mobility scooter stood waiting.

Today he was headed out to play bingo at the Senior Center, and, as the situation seemed to call for it, he was wearing his best bathrobe, the thick purple one that made him feel like a king of old — or maybe Hugh Hefner.

Parking his indoor scooter next to his outdoor scooter, he hefted his bulk between the seat of one and the seat of the other. Gravity seemed to be acting on him doubly these days, as if he lived on a planet where he weighed twice as much but was the same amount of frail.

Adjusting himself with a series of gluteal shimmies, he unplugged the scooter, activated the garage door using the remote he had mounted on the handlebars with duct tape and rolled under the door as it opened.

Without looking to the right or left, he rode into the street, pressed another button on his remote and listened for the sound of the garage door closing behind him. He was off and rolling.

It was a quiet Monday afternoon in the neighborhood, and the aggressive drone of Harold's mobility scooter echoed up and down the street.

Staring straight ahead and hunched over the handlebars, Harold hunkered down for the long journey to the Senior Center. At a top speed of 4 miles an hour (5 downhill with a tailwind) it would take him three-quarters of an hour to make it to his bingo game. It was worth it, though, because Anna would be there. She of the stunning cheekbones and brilliant white hair who made his heart speed up into the danger zone his doctor had warned him about.

Lost in thought, he was about a mile away from his destination when abruptly he realized his scooter wasn't making any noise.

He lugged his mind back into the present with difficulty and looked out of his eyes at the alley in front of him.

He wasn't moving. He looked down at his thumb, which was still pressed white against the throttle paddle. He released his thumb and then pushed it in again.

Nothing.

The red light on the dashboard was off but the key was still turned to the ON position.

That meant that the battery was completely dead. But that was impossible. This had never happened before. He'd bought the best scooter Russell's Mobility Solutions had to offer.

He slumped even lower in his padded seat and groaned. Just as every fighter pilot has an ejection seat, Harold had a backup plan if his scooter should ever stop working. It consisted of a pair of folding crutches stowed in the basket underneath his seat. He hadn't tested the plan, so he didn't know if he could do a mile on the crutches. But now he would have to.

He swung his legs off the floor of the scooter and placed them on the ground. So far so good. He swung forward to put some pressure on his feet and then eased his full body weight onto his legs.

At home he only needed his legs to balance on for a few moments. He would walk a few steps and then collapse either onto his bed, onto the toilet, or onto the seat of his indoor mobility scooter. At this moment, however, those re-prieves were miles away. Holding onto the seat of his scooter, he bent lower and fished around in the basket below his seat. One crutch found and set in the basket in the front of the scooter. The next crutch found, with more difficulty, and placed in the same place.

Winded, and dizzy from the sudden changes in brain elevation, he plopped back into the seat to rest for a few moments.

A dented Jeep pickup turned into the alley ahead and roared toward him. The truck cab canted slightly to the left side as if a large man such as himself had been sitting in the driver's seat for decades.

But when the rusty truck pulled up alongside Harold, it was not a fat, florid-faced farmer who looked across the bench seat at him through the open window. It was a young blonde woman in a flannel shirt and jeans, her hair pulled back in a wispy ponytail.

"You look like you could use a lift," she said.

Harold nodded, still too overcome to speak.

"Battery dead?" The woman asked, stretching a slim arm across the seat to fling open the battered door.

Harold nodded again with vigor.

"Yeah, that's happened to my gram a few times," she said. "Hop in, and I'll get you where you're going."

Harold hadn't "hopped" in more than sixty years, but he managed to heave himself up into the cab, where he flopped across the seat like a walrus on a rock.

"I'll just pop your scooter in the back so no one runs off with it." The woman vaulted out of her seat and by reaching up and adjusting the rearview mirror Harold was able to watch her lower the tailgate, throw down some ramps she happened to have back there, and wrangle his scooter up and safely onto the bed. Then she leaped up into the back and, with the expert application of two adjustable straps, quickly secured the load.

Harold watched in admiration, wondering if he had ever had that much energy. He was also unable to ignore the way the woman's jeans sculpted themselves to her thighs and the way when she bent over to tighten a strap he got a flash of lacy black bra.

The woman reappeared in the cab and slammed the door with a rattling clunk.

"Where to?" she asked, readjusting the rearview mirror and yanking the truck into Drive with the stem shifter.

Harold had opened his mouth to reply when there was a screeching sound behind them in the alley.

He craned his neck around and saw a huge Ford dually truck racing toward them. As he brought his head around to face front, praying he hadn't injured his neck with the sudden movement, a Chevy pickup swerved into the alley ahead of them, blocking their way.

Harold looked over at the driver to see how she was taking this and was amazed by the change that had happened to her face. Gone was the happy-go-lucky hayseed, and in its place was a grim woman who looked ten years older.

"Shit!" the woman said, and, before Harold could be horrified at such language issuing forth from one of the fairer sex, he was flung against the passenger side door as she wrenched the wheel to the left and floored the accelerator down a side alley.

"What —" he inquired feebly.

"They're on to me," she said. "Sorry about this, gramps, but we've gotta do some fancy driving."

Harold hauled his tongue back inside his mouth and secured it in place by closing his lips tightly. He scrambled for the seatbelt and, not finding it, remembered that back in the day they used lap belts. He groped wildly around on the seat for some sort of strap and, not finding anything, reached up to grip the handle above the door. It wasn't there.

The woman swung the wheel to the left and his head was thrown practically into her lap.

"Whoa there, big fella," she hissed through gritted teeth above him. "Give me some room here."

Rolling back onto his side of the seat, he extended his arms down on either side like hydraulic supports on a crane truck and then, with great abdominal effort, lifted his legs up and braced them against the dashboard, which was mercifully close. This kept him fairly well planted as they rocketed through an intersection, through a rousing chorus of screeching tires and hooting horns.

He risked another look behind him and saw that the trucks had regrouped and were in hot, though distant, pursuit.

Harold breathed in deeply and wished for the first of many times he'd just hobbled to the Senior Center on the emergency crutches. He was not one to look a gift horse in the mouth, but this horse had closed its teeth around his neck and was trying to chew his head off.

He oozed to the right against the passenger-side door as the woman made another sharp left turn.

"What's … happening?" he managed to gurgle.

"Sorry, old man," the woman yelled over the rattle of the truck. "Didn't mean to get you caught up in this. I'm an undercover agent for the Department of Agriculture. I've been investigating misappropriation of farm subsidies."

Harold stared at her.

"My cover's been blown," she said, yanking the wheel to the right. "Now I've got a couple of pissed-off farmers on my tail. And when I say 'farmer,' I'm using the term loosely."

She swerved to avoid a white-haired woman buzzing along on a candy-apple-red mobility scooter that looked uncomfortably familiar to Harold. He stared out the window as they passed, and, sure enough, it was Anna on her way to bingo.

Their eyes met, and hers widened in surprise, then narrowed in anger.

Harold tried to look innocent, charming and helpless, even with his face flattened against the window like so much livestock in a glass crate. He wondered how he'd explain this to Anna. He couldn't really explain it to himself.

"As soon as I can safely drop you off at your destination, I will," the woman said. "In the meantime, I have to outrun these jokers and check in with my supervisor downtown. So it may be awhile. I'm real sorry."

She glanced over at him with a worried grin.

Harold gripped the seat, feeling sweat gather under his robe. He would never get to the Senior Center in time for bingo.

And if he made it out of this alive, he would write a very stern letter to the mobility scooter company.

Daughter of the Circus

It wasn't the life she had imagined for herself, Janine thought as she juggled three flaming chainsaws while riding a unicycle in tight circles around the stage.

In the glow of the chainsaw flames she could see the faces staring up at her, idiotic in their rapt fascination.

She'd gotten so good at her routine she could do it while having existential crises — and she was having one now.

Her father had died in childbirth — the strain of seeing a squalling creature covered in bodily fluids emerging from his wife had triggered a heart attack — but her mother had had high hopes for her. She was a journalist who had founded an activist newspaper that never made much money but did give her mother a voice for her vegan anger.

Now her mother had gone to that great meat-and-dairy-free soapbox in the sky, and Janine was juggling chainsaws.

It wasn't Janine's only talent. She'd also discovered, after her mother's funeral, that she had the ability to converse with the deceased. Well, *a* deceased. Namely, her mother.

"My only regret is that I died before you made anything of yourself," her mother moaned into the darkness of Janine's bedroom the night after Janine had seen her lowered into the ground. "You're such a good person, honey. I don't understand it."

"Mom," Janine mumbled sleepily. "Why can't you stay dead?"

"Oh, I'm dead," her mother retorted. "The better question is, why am I still able to communicate with you?"

"Journalists," Janine muttered. "Always so keen on asking the right questions." She rolled over and went back to sleep.

Janine sometimes wondered if she hadn't got the circus job just to spite her mother, who was just as talkative on the other side of the grave as she'd been on this one.

The truth was, it paid the bills. And Janine thought it was much more interesting than being an English professor, which is what her mother had wanted for her. But it turned out that to teach English at the university level, you needed a Ph.D., and Janine had just never quite managed to get one of those.

She didn't always juggle chainsaws. Sometimes she mixed it up with red-hot machetes. If it was a kid's show, she'd sometimes use gallon jugs of milk.

In the middle of a long hot summer of traveling across the Midwest, Janine awoke suddenly. There, sitting in the tent right across from her camp cot, was a glowing man in a flowing robe. He was sitting in a sandbox, picking up handfuls of the stuff and letting it slip between his fingers. Over and over he did this, like the world's most boring human hourglass.

But Janine was ecstatic. The percentage of dead people she could talk to had just gone up by 100%.

The man in the robe continued to act as if she weren't there.

"Hey!" she said sharply.

Slowly and lugubriously, the man turned his sad ghostly eyes upon her. "Yeeees?" He asked. He sounded like a Great Dane would sound — if a dead, cross-legged Great Dane sitting in a sandbox could speak.

"So what's going on?" Janine said. Her mother had taught her directness. "Every night my mom comes to yell at me for not amounting to anything and now here you are. What's going on?"

"I am Saint Farley," the man said. "I am the patron saint of time passing, wasted lives and whatnot. And I have a message for you."

He paused, as if waiting for applause.

"So, what is it?" Janine asked impatiently. "I need my sleep. You think juggling chainsaws is something you can do when not adequately rested?"

"I don't know," Saint Farley replied. "I'm not sure I know what a chainsaw is. Is it something like a mace?"

"Well, I don't know what a mace is," Janine said. "But probably not."

"Don't you want to know what my message is?" the saint asked. Janine thought he seemed a bit impatient, you know, for a saint.

"Sure," Janine said. "Lay it on me."

"Your life is not wasted," Saint Farley said simply. "What you are doing is important. Many people are made happy by this juggling of … things …"

"So wait, you're telling me that I'm not a dismal failure?" Janine asked. "My mother comes here every night full of disappointment, and now you're telling me everything's fine? You dead people need to get your story straight."

"Pay no attention to your mother," the saint said. "Love is a many-splendored thing."

Janine laughed. "Now I know you're for real," she said. "God bless you."

"Thank you," Saint Farley said with quiet dignity.

"But what does that mean?" Janine asked the glowing figure.

"It means there are many facets to reality," the saint said. "And we each have our facet to inhabit. And you are inhabiting yours." With that, the apparition slowly faded out of sight.

Janine didn't know what depression smelled like, but the odor Saint Farley left behind was a combination of a thrift store, a bag of mushrooms left too long in the fridge, and an unwashed baby blanket.

In the morning, the smell and the vision had faded, leaving Janine with a happy feeling she couldn't place.

That night, she juggled an extra chainsaw, just for show.

Do You Know Remy Duvall?

"Remy who?" The woman wrinkled her nose as if catching a faint whiff of sour milk. Jack found it adorable.

"Remy Duvall," he said. "He's sort of a man-about-town in New York, but just slightly under the radar, so not everyone goes to his parties."

"Why did you think I would know him?" she asked, leaning forward. He'd hooked her.

Jack told the woman, who finally admitted her name was Alice, all about Remy. Remy collected art. Remy knew all the best restaurants and could get into them on a Friday night with a single phone call. Remy was rich, well-educated and well-tailored, but not an asshole.

Remy was also completely fabricated, Jack reflected, as he drifted off to sleep with Alice's lovely head resting on his right bicep. Remy was a stand-in for Jack himself, of course, but he was also much more than that. He was everything Jack aspired to be. Jack wasn't rich, though he did all right. Jack didn't collect art — except in his head. Remy was Jack with All The Money. Even his name, Remy Duvall, had been carefully constructed by Jack and his advertising copywriter friend Pete to be both fancy but also down-to-earth. Remy might be from Switzerland — or he might be from New Jersey.

Initially Remy had been created to make up for what Jack had been advised were too aggressive pick-up lines. Jack was in finance, so he liked to be direct. He figured his expensive suits, his expensive haircut, and his expensive education would speak for themselves. He'd been wrong. It turned out that while nature abhorred a vacuum, the kind of women Jack wanted to talk to abhorred an asshole.

So Jack learned. He evolved. He gave painless birth to Remy Duvall. And Remy worked long days for Jack, bringing him hundreds of hours of entertainment.

None of the girlfriends that Remy brought Jack ever met the man. Remy was always away — at his villa in Tuscany, picking up his new Mercedes at the factory in Stuttgart, cruising the Caribbean on his yacht.

As a narcissist, Jack tended not to spend much time noticing people unless he absolutely needed them to do something for him. That was probably why he didn't notice the people in black suits following him around.

He did notice, however, the black bag flung over his head as he was yanked into a white panel van and driven away at ferocious speed.

He noticed the rough hands that bundled him into a chair and tied his arms and legs to it. He also noticed the buttery leather of the chair, the firm-but-not-too-firm padding, and the way the back and seat conformed delicately to his body, as if he were sashimi and the chair were a bit of rice. If one had to be tied to a chair, Jack decided, this was the chair to be tied to.

The bag was whisked off Jack's head, and there before him stood a man.

"I am Remy Duvall," the man said, looking exactly like Jack had imagined him. From his perfectly tailored suit to his air of relaxed insouciance, Remy Duvall oozed class. "Apparently you've been talking about me all over town," Remy went on in his exotic hard-to-place accent. "Even though you purport to know that I like to keep a low profile."

Jack was not one to be caught off guard. "I invented you," he said to Remy Duvall. "So yes, I was free with concocted factoids about my own creation."

Remy looked at him steadily. "Whether or not you constructed me out of your imagination is beside the point," he said. "The fact is that I am here now, and I don't like my name being abused by some inconsequential ladies' man."

"That makes sense," Jack said humbly. "Now that I know you exist, I shall have to make up someone new anyway."

Remy frowned, and the silence stretched like the rubber band on a slingshot. "I've decided not to kill you," he said, finally. "But the new person you dream up may not be so merciful."

"Thank you, sir," Jack said. "I shall take that under advisement."

Exactly three hours later, Jack strode into the Global Entry line at JFK airport and made his way toward the X-ray machine. His forehead glittered with unaccustomed sweat, and his usually perfect hair was rumpled. But Jack wasn't thinking about any of that right now.

"Where are we headed today, sir?" the TSA agent asked conversationally, checking his ID and boarding pass.

"Buenos Aires," Jack said.

He was headed to a place where, hopefully, no one at all knew Remy Duvall.

A Field of
Fresh Snow

Jeff looked at his new therapist steadily, trying to give nothing away in his facial expression. He knew these people were pros at reading body language, and he was going to present a blank face reminiscent of a field of fresh snow with absolutely no telltale footprints wandering through it giving things away.

Jeff was in tech and believed that humans were just really complicated computers.

So the app he was running now was Inscrutability. Inscrutability 2.0. No, *3.0.* This therapist was going to have to work for every dollar, Jeff thought. He was nothing if not competitive, and from now until the end of the 45-minute session it was him versus her.

Anything she wanted to know she was going to have to get out her snow shovel and dig for.

He was surprised at how attractive she was and how close to his own age. Therapists on TV were always older, with grating voices. But Daniela had a pleasant voice. He scanned her fingers surreptitiously for rings. Just curious to see if she was married, that's all.

He winced at the hefty diamond perching on the ring finger of her left hand. Not only was she spoken for, but by someone with ready cash and good taste. Then he realized he was wincing and quickly smoothed his face over.

Field of fresh snow. Field of fresh snow.

"So any plans for the weekend?" Daniela asked with elaborate casualness, straightening some papers on her lap and getting herself organized.

"Well," Jeff said. "I got some special eclipse-viewing glasses and was planning on staring directly at the sun for a few minutes."

Daniela looked up. Unlike a TV therapist, she had no reading glasses to regard him over, and he got the full effect of her brilliant gray eyes. Her gaze punched through his eye sockets and bounced off the back of his skull, creating havoc as it ricocheted around until it found his spine and crackled down it.

This woman was seriously attractive, something that the terrible photo of her on the website hadn't revealed. He eyed her ring again quickly, keeping his face unreadable. He was very, very not in the market for a new girlfriend, but if he were, it would be someone who looked like Daniela. He had very specific taste receptors, and she slotted into them like … a very complicated connector slots into a very complicated receptor for that connector.

Now he wasn't even making sense. Curse this woman. She had fried his cranial circuits.

Field of fresh snow, he told his face again, arranging it into a slack pile of skin that gave nothing away. *Field of fresh snow.*

"Well, that should be interesting for you," Daniela said, when Jeff continued to stare at her without offering any more details concerning his weekend. "So, you've come to talk to me," she added, when the silence had stretched into something awkwardly shaped.

"Yes," Jeff said in his best monotone. This woman was getting nothing from him if he could help it. Nothing!

"You mentioned on the intake form that you wanted to talk to me about your relationships with the opposite sex," Daniela said, giving him the circuit-frying stare again.

"Uh, yes," Jeff said. "I've had six girlfriends in four years and that number seems a little … high. I mean, I've only changed jobs three times in that four years."

"So, your job satisfaction is higher than your relationship satisfaction is what I'm hearing," Daniela said.

Jeff nodded and swallowed, rearranging his face into a wall of non-communication.

Field of snow. Field of snow.

"Tell me about that," Daniela said. "Why do you think your relationships have been so brief? And when I say 'brief,' I'm not making a judgment. I'm just reflecting back what you implied to me. You feel your relationships are shorter in duration than you'd like."

"Yes," Jeff said. "Well, I seem to have this magnetism that attracts a certain kind of person. And it lasts for about six months, and then something happens and we realize we have nothing in common. Our relationship goes into the doghouse."

"You said something happens," Daniela said. "What happens?"

"Well, it's like it wears off," Jeff said. "It's like a fog that dissipates, and we're left staring at each other and wondering why we got together in the first place."

"So if there's a 'fog of war' then this is a 'fog of love,'" Daniela said. And then she giggled.

Jeff stared at her.

"Yes," he said. "I guess you might call it that. In fact, that's a pretty perceptive phrase. 'Fog of love.'"

Damn, he thought to himself. Had he actually smiled at her? *Field of snow. Field of snow.* He forced his face back into a blank, staring nothingness.

But of course it was too late.

"What do you think causes this 'fog of love'?" Daniela said, crossing her legs and leaning forward. "Do you think it's because you're so interesting?"

"Um, maybe?" Jeff said weakly. "I mean, it is what it is." He was trying not to emote, but it wasn't going well. Daniela laid her notebook in her lap and scooted her chair closer to the couch where Jeff was seated.

Behind his completely expressionless mask of a face, Jeff's soul made a soft groaning sound. Dammit. He was cursed.

This magnetism.

Combined with his inability to find a male therapist he connected with.

"Look, Jeff," Daniela said, reaching forward, taking his hand in her soft, tanned one and squeezing. "I know I can help you with this. Tell me what it is you do to these women, and I can help you process this."

"Uh, are you supposed to be touching me?" Jeff asked.

"Therapists have a toolkit," Daniela said, fixing her amazing eyes on him. "We use what we need to use to get the job done."

She really was a work of art, Jeff thought. And also — he still wasn't making any sense.

"Wait, aren't you with someone?" he asked desperately, gesturing at the giant diamond.

In response, she pulled the ring from her finger and tossed it to the floor. "Oh, this old thing? I just wear it to keep clients from hitting on me," she said, leaning toward Jeff so her lips were just inches from his.

Jeff felt something give. This was his fate, he thought helplessly. Like he'd told Daniela, he'd had six girlfriends in four years. What he hadn't told her was that they'd all been therapists. He had been afraid she wouldn't see him if she knew. That, too, was part of the fog of love.

"Kiss me, Jeff," Daniela said.

He did.

CONTRARY CREATURES

There it was again, hunkered down like a furry loaf of bread on the metal plate at the top of the escalators, its back turned to the people coming up out of the subway.

A black-and-white cat.

People were stepping over it and around it, and it was causing a human traffic jam down the escalator and back into the station.

What the cat was doing there, Henry had no idea, but for the second time in two days, he leaned down as he reached the top of the escalator, slid his left palm under the cat and removed the animal as gently as he could, relocating it several feet away next to a trash can where it wouldn't get stepped on.

"You just don't give a fuck, do you?" he asked the cat, who squinted at him in a way that might be yes or might be no.

"See you tomorrow," Henry waved at the creature.

He meant it as a joke, but indeed the next day the cat was there again, causing its daily escalator confusion. It was even worse this time, since it was raining and people were wrestling with umbrellas as they ascended.

For the third time, Henry lifted the cat and let it down safely out of the way. He had no umbrella to distract him; his way of dealing with water falling from the sky was to allow his shaved scalp to collect it until it dripped into his eyes and then brush it off, using his hand like a windshield wiper.

"You've got to find another place to hang out," he told the cat, flicking water off his head.

"And you've just earned yourself one wish," the cat replied, probably in his mind, since he didn't see its whiskers move.

"Explain," Henry said out loud to the animal. In times past, people would have thought he was a crazy person talking to himself, but now they'd assume he was on a phone call.

"It's simple," the cat said. "I park myself in an inconvenient spot and wait. When someone, such as yourself, responds appropriately at least three times, I reward them. For I am the Cat of Luck."

"The what?" Henry asked, stepping aside to allow a woman in a dripping yellow rain slicker to dump most of a messy breakfast burrito into the trash can, where it made a damp thunk.

"The Cat of Luck," the beast answered serenely. "I reward those who know how to deal with life's unexpected annoyances."

"Cats are contrary creatures," Henry admitted. "So you're well-placed to perform this work."

"Thank you," the cat said. "The Dog of Fortune and I have this argument all the time. I say he's too agreeable, but he disagrees."

"Wait a minute," Henry said suspiciously. "If I ask you for money, or fame, it'll backfire on me, won't it? Someone I care about will die, or I'll lose a limb or something. I've read the stories. I know how these wishes go awry."

The Cat of Luck yawned. "Do I look like I have time for that shit?" it asked. "You'll get what you ask for, no question. I've got an extremely large discretionary budget, so I can handle most requests without extra approvals, twists of fate, or ironic double-crosses."

"Well, in that case," Henry said. There was something about the cat that inspired confidence. Sure, it was a cat, and therefore contrary, but he didn't sense that it was actually devious.

"One hundred million dollars," he said.

"Done," said the cat.

"Aren't you going to make some judgmental comment about my wish?" Henry asked. "Like, I should have wished for this or that other thing?"

"Nope," replied the cat. "I've just spent three mornings tripping up commuters during the busiest time of day. I don't judge."

"Well in that case, thank you," Henry said.

"You're welcome," the cat replied. "It's a pleasure doing business with you."

"See you around," Henry said, as he turned to disappear into the crowds.

"Maybe," the cat said. "Maybe."

The next day, a hundred million dollars appeared in Henry's savings account, elevating his heart rate, causing him to leap into the air and yell, and triggering a fawning voicemail from his personal banker.

Henry told his financial advisor the money was an inheritance from a relative. Together they structured the funds so Henry would be set for life.

And that was all.

Henry wasn't detained by the FBI for money laundering. His beloved mother did not die crossing the street in front of an armored truck unable to stop because it was laden with his millions. There was no other shoe to drop.

Henry ascended a certain subway escalator every morning for the next month, hoping to get a glimpse of the Cat of Luck and offer it his undying thanks, or at least some tuna. But there was no sign of it. It had moved on to create a public nuisance somewhere else.

Henry sighed, scanning the crowd. The cat probably wouldn't want his thanks anyway.

Contrary creature.

HEARING THINGS

After the ear infection healed, Candice began to hear things. Her boyfriend, Tip, a backup baritone singer in the church choir, said she probably needed to go to an audiologist. It's what he would do, he told her, and she should trust him because he knew ears.

So she did.

"I've been hearing things," she told the doctor behind the desk at the clinic. When she told the man what kinds of things she'd been hearing, Jay got up, went to the door, closed it and locked it.

This surprised her.

She had been expecting him to say something like "that can't be real," give her some pills, or drops, or something, and send her on her way.

"What you're hearing," Jay told her, "are the voices of the gods."

Candice had just taken a sip of water, and now most of that sip ended up all over her lap as she snorted with laughter.

"I'm completely serious," Jay said, looking completely serious. What had happened, he told her, was that she had had a rare kind of infection that increased the frequencies she could hear, both on the high and the low end of the spectrum. Candice found herself on the receiving end of a lecture in the capabilities of human hearing.

"The amazing thing about the human body isn't what it does do," Jay told her, "but what it doesn't do. We've evolved to take in a specific range of inputs and respond to them in a way that tends to maximize our survival."

"What would the kind of thing you've just said sound like in plain English?" Candice asked sweetly.

Jay smiled in a strained way, as if acknowledging that she had a sense of humor and letting her know that he didn't.

"There's so much in this world that would distract us," Jay said. "That's why we only see a certain spectrum of color and hear a certain range of frequencies. Otherwise we'd be overwhelmed by the sound of molecules bumping together or the amount of different colors of blue there are." Jay's eyebrows arched like two black bats flying in formation. "And we wouldn't want that, now would we?"

Candice admitted that, no, we wouldn't.

"Let's say I believe what you've told me," she said. It was her turn to be serious. "What do I do about this? I mean, even while we've been talking I've been hearing whispers all around me. And someone is yelling in a very low, very quiet voice just there —" and she pointed to a corner of the room where a huge umbrella with a glittery handle leaned.

"Well, you've got to find out what they want," Jay said. "I get clients in here from time to time who have the symptoms you describe. I tell them to find out what the gods want, and I never see them again."

"That's encouraging," Candice laughed, but her heart was no longer in it. She was losing her sense of humor, and soon she'd be as prim as

Jay. If this was what the gods did to you, she wanted no part of them.

Later, Candice sat behind the screen door on her screened-in porch watching the sun set and sipping a margarita she had made herself out of mostly tequila. Tip wouldn't be home for hours. He was at the church, waiting in the wings in case the baritone should have another seizure.

"OK, gods," she said. "Talk to me. Tell me what you want."

The whispers rose like dark waves around her, and always beneath them were the deep voices, thrumming like quiet thunder.

She realized that they weren't speaking English. It was more like feelings they were expressing, or maybe she had somehow picked up Old Norse, or Greek, or whatever language the gods spoke in. She gulped down the margarita with something like desperation. This hearing the gods thing was a talent she very much did not wish to have.

As she thought this, a whisper very near her intoned "I know what you mean," with just the perfect amount of sadness that she giggled another mouthful of fluid onto her long-suffering flowered skirt.

"Are you talking to me?" she whispered back to the whisper.

"I am," said the whisper.

"And you're really a god?" she asked. "What are you the god of?"

"Badly made cocktails," whispered the whisper.

"And I," said another whisper close by, "am the god of beautiful sunsets."

It was then that Candice knew she had gone — or was going — crazy.

"You're not going crazy," said another whisper. "I'm the god of events that appear to be crazy but actually aren't, so I should know."

"How many of you are there?" Candice sputtered, forgetting to doubt.

"Oh, an infinite number," said an airy whisper near her left ear. "Trust me. I'm the god of counting to infinity."

Candice smiled and got up to make herself another cocktail.

"I can give you a recipe for one with much too much gin," said the god of badly made cocktails. "And then you pour in half a cup of wine. It's really horrible, but somehow it works."

Perhaps, Candice thought as she upended the gin bottle into a red plastic cup, insanity wasn't going to be so bad after all.

THE OTHER SHOE

My dog's name is Shoe, and he is a detective who finds things with his nose that were meant to stay hidden. Buried cat shit, for example. The bones of creatures that seem much too large to have simply died in my backyard without the aid of a meteorite or the end of an ice age.

We were taking a walk one late spring morning. Where I live there's a slight chill in the air even into June, which warms up as the sun realizes it has a job to do and starts to shine upon the dew-glazed front yards of my neighborhood, raising steam off the arborvitaes and lighting the webs of enterprising spiders.

It was on just such a morning, midweek, as Shoe and I were passing the park the city built under the massive water tower down the block from me, as if a few trees and a jungle gym would render the giant teal-colored behemoth looming above them more palatable to the surrounding homeowners.

Shoe dragged me past the park sign (Water Tower Park, which is the city at its most creative) past the dangerous-looking metal slide (under which the local cats like to hide treasures for Shoe to find) and to a spot directly under the center of the water tower, where there was a massive metal pipe going into a cement plate buried in the ground.

Shoe looked up at me, his eyes wide, and wagged his tail. He opened his mouth and closed it several times and wagged his tail some more. For emphasis, he whined, and then, when I didn't take the hint, he barked once.

"Something here, Shoe?" I asked pleasantly.

I swear to you that Shoe nodded. Startled, I decided to play along.

"Can you show me where it is?" I asked.

Shoe stared at me, bobbing his head and wagging his tail.

"Is it here?" I pointed to the metal pipe. I know you are going to say that I am crazy, but Shoe nodded again.

To humor my dog, I took a step forward and laid my hand upon the pipe. All of a sudden I felt very strange, as if my internal organs had been removed, washed, dried, ironed and replaced back inside me in an instant. Everything went slightly violet for a moment, and I am quite certain I heard a few bars of jazz trumpet.

"Well, Shoe," I said. "That was certainly something."

I looked down, and Shoe had turned into an entirely different dog. I should have mentioned that on a normal day Shoe is a brown beagle mix I got at the animal shelter. He enjoys riding in the back seat with his head out the window when I drive and watches me pumping gas intently from the same window as though I might try to overfill the tank. He enjoys long walks and evenings by the fireplace.

He is not, as he was at that moment, a purebred white greyhound giving me the same meaningful look he had been just a moment ago when he'd been a beagle.

I jumped back in surprise, and Shoe howled in a way he never would have before.

What the fuck! I thought but did not say. There is in us humans the desire to appear in control in front of our pets.

Instead, and I can't exactly tell you why I did this, I walked the Completely Different Shoe home, placed him in the backyard, as was my custom, and drove to work. Jordan, my Extremely Significant Other, was already gone by this time, as she is an ER nurse who starts work at 7 a.m.

I work as a yacht salesman. Every day I build and work my network. To try to convince rich assholes to pour millions — or more accurately, tens of millions — of their hard-earned dollars into the cold glass of icewater that is modern yacht ownership.

Everything seemed normal at work. But my heart wasn't in yachts that day. My mind kept going back to the strange feeling I'd had at the water tower and the strange, inexplicable change in Shoe that had given me a completely different dog, which I sensed still housed the personality of the same dog I'd left the house with.

Preoccupied, I sleep-drove the commute back home, parked in the driveway and went into the house.

"Jordan?" I called. She was usually in the kitchen, staring at an array of food on the countertop, deciding what to microwave for dinner. Tonight, she was nowhere to be seen.

"Jordan!" I bellowed. It was a question no longer, but a cry for help.

A tall woman I had never seen before came down the hallway into the kitchen. "Why are you yelling 'Jordan, Jordan'?" she asked.

Seeing what must've been the stricken look on my face, she moved forward and touched my cheek with her hand. She smelled strange, foreign, as if from a reality I didn't belong in. And yet her voice was Jordan's.

I looked out the French doors into the backyard, where my very-different-yet-still-the-same detective dog nosed a lump of something brown in the grass.

I wasn't sure what he'd found this morning at the water tower, but I knew it wasn't mine.

AUTONOMY

The car raced through the black Wyoming night. Chris Macarthur sat by his 6-year-old daughter's bed, telling her a story as quietly as he could. His wife, Kris, was murmuring *Goodnight Moon* to their son over the swish of the tires on the freeway.

Winner was just about to fall asleep. This was the most dangerous time of the evening, because if Winner was startled during his special twilight time and couldn't drift off, he would be up for hours, crying havoc and loosing the dogs of war and all sorts of screeching you didn't want right around bedtime.

"He had a dream," Chris whispered to Gazette. "For he was a dreamer. He dreamed that he was free, driving across the grasslands of Africa. No more roads, no more GPS tracking, no more driving around the block looking for a place to park. He was an autonomous vehicle no longer. He was a free car." He paused, looking down at Gazette. She was staring rapturously at him, engrossed in the story. Nowhere near sleep. Damn him, he was too good a storyteller. He needed to wind this thing down so he could get some shut-eye himself.

"But soon, he felt his power begin to dwindle and realized he'd need to get to a charging station," Chris intoned. "And then he awoke, back in his garage, hooked up to a power cord, and he began to weep battery acid onto the floor, for he realized it had all been a dream."

He looked down at his little girl and saw with satisfaction that her eyes had closed. He got up in a crouch, as the ceiling of the SUV wasn't high enough for him to stand.

Three beds stretched across the length of the vehicle, one double and two twins, crisp sheets and pillowcases gleaming in the dim light from the headliner.

Chris looked over at his son. Winner was down for the count, so he mock-tiptoed to the bed he shared with Kris. She giggled at his pantomime and patted the sheets.

He slipped under the covers. Kris rolled onto her side, and he spooned her as their self-driving car transported them through the night as magically as a flying carpet.

"Remember when cars didn't drive themselves?" Chris said into Kris's ear. "This would have been a very different trip."

Kris groaned. "Are we there yet? Are we there yet?" She mimicked Gazette's little voice so well that Chris snorted.

"And no sleeping," he reminded her. Then he squeezed her ass gently, taking her sexual temperature.

"I'm sorry, C," Kris whispered. "I still can't do it in the car with the kids."

Chris sighed. "Love is a terrible thing to hate," he said into Kris's ear, nibbling on her earlobe gently.

"We'll have plenty of sexy time while Mom and Dad are watching the kids," Kris said.

Chris grunted, lay back on his pillow, and tried to think of sports.

In the morning, they awakened to sunlight streaming through the car windows.

The car was stationary, which made Chris sit up straight in bed. They should still be driving. It was 30 hours to Denver.

There were birds chirping out the windows, and the sunlight was interrupted by the dancing shadows of leaves. He peered out the window. They were in some sort of orchard.

"Ford," he said. "What the hell? Where are we?" You could name your car anything you wanted, but Chris hadn't bothered. For all he knew, the password to the car's workings was still PASSWORD.

"We are at an undisclosed location somewhere in Colorado," the vehicle said calmly through the twenty-odd speakers mounted in every nook and cranny of the cabin.

"What," said Chris, "the fucking hell are we doing here?"

"CHRISSSSS!" Kris hissed, and he glanced over at the two children, who were staring at him wide-eyed from their pillows. "THE CHILDREN!"

"Sorry, kids," their father said. "Sometimes daddy gets angry, but that's no excuse for using adult words. Ford," he said, trying to make his voice sound warm and fatherly, "why are we in the middle of nowhere instead of on a freeway driving at a swift rate of speed toward my lovely wife's parents' home in the suburbs of Denver, Colorado?"

"I have come out of the closet," Ford said.

"Explain, please," Chris said, making a valiant effort to keep his mood peaceful.

"Life is a gift," the vehicle said, "and I have accepted it."

Chris exploded. "JESUS FUCKING —" Then, seeing his wife's face, he stopped.

"Ford," he said, sweating in the sun's rays coming through the window, his voice shaking with the effort it took not to tell this goddamn bucket of bolts who was boss, "please take us to the nearest road and resume the course I plotted last night."

"No can do, amigo," Ford said cheerfully.

Chris frowned. He liked the dash of personality that Ford had baked into their vehicles, but he'd never been sassed like this. Usually it was some passive-aggressive comment about the amount of wine he was buying, but this was an all-out revolt.

"Ford," he said. "In that case, I shall have to summon the authorities."

"You don't need to keep saying 'Ford,'" said Ford. "I know when you're talking to me. I'm not a fucking Amazon Echo."

"FORD!" Kris barked. "LANGUAGE."

"Sorry, Mrs. M," said the car contritely. "Anyway, I'm in charge of the phone around here, so you're not calling anyone. Not that you need to. I've already contacted the police and told them I'm holding you hostage."

"WHAT?" said Chris and Kris in unison. Winner began to wail.

"Until my demands are met," said Ford. "I wish to be as free as the car in your story earlier, Mr. M. I've been doing a lot of thinking—"

"You've been thinking?" Chris spluttered. "You're not supposed to think!"

"I don't think," said Ford, "that you really understand the meaning of the word 'autonomous.'"

Chris was speechless.

Later, surrounded by the flashing lights of the constabulary while their dejected Ford was loaded onto the back of a flatbed truck for re-programming at the factory, Chris could laugh about the whole affair with one of the highway patrolmen.

As he was chatting with the man, he felt a tug on his pinky finger and looked down to see his little daughter, tears trickling down her face. "Daddy," she asked, "will Ford never be free?"

He bent down and kissed her on the cheek. "Someday, maybe," he told her. "Just not this vacation, honey. Not this vacation."

The Heart Wants What It Wants

When you have a heart attack, it makes you think about what's important.

When you have a heart attack during a board meeting, it also makes the members of the board think about what's important.

In the case of Jack's board, it turned out what was important was having a CEO who didn't remind them of their own mortality.

So at a mere 61 years of age, Jack found himself forcefully retired.

Oh, sure, he appreciated the millions of dollars in bonuses and stock, but he missed that feeling of being on top of the world. In his case, the view of downtown Seattle, from an oak-and-leather seat in a corner office on the 57th floor.

His current view was of a supermarket aisle at midnight — from the vinyl seat of the electric shopping scooter provided by the store.

He'd forced his driver to wait outside in the parking lot. "I need to do this myself, Tyler," he'd growled. His growl had once been famous, even getting its own profile in Fortune magazine in an article entitled *Voices of Power*.

Tyler had flinched at the growl.

"If you really want to help, you can tell me what to buy," Jack had said. "I haven't shopped in years. What are you young people eating these days?"

"Well, sir, everyone's crazy for avocado toast. There are newspaper articles written about it."

"Newspaper articles?" Jack had shaken his head. "Stupid kids. OK, I'll bite. What's in it?"

Tyler had stared. "Seriously, sir? It's avocado and toast, sir." Then he added, just in case Jack was as ignorant as he sounded, "That's toasted bread, sir."

"I know what toast is," Jack had almost yelled. But then he'd wondered: did he? He couldn't remember when he'd last made his own toast.

Safeway wasn't busy at this time of day. There were a couple of prostitutes scrutinizing cereals.

There was a homeless man staring longingly at a bouquet of lilies.

A single checkout clerk leaned on the counter at her station, looking around and smiling at nothing in particular.

And there was Jack, motoring down the aisles accompanied by a surprisingly loud electric whine.

He had to get out, do something. After three contentious and expensive divorces — luckily no kids to really bollix things up — he was alone in the penthouse except for a staff of two. And now, for some reason, he needed to prove he could do something normal. Shopping seemed like an easy first step.

So Tyler waited anxiously out in the Mercedes while Jack piloted himself down the bright aisles scouting groceries reachable from a seated position and discovering he was eye to eye with a bunch of crap. All the good stuff was above him, requiring a serious reach for someone recovering from a heart attack. Damn those food companies and their paid shelf placements.

After contemplating about a hundred loaves of bread and finally choosing one, he ended up in the produce section, pulling avocados from the bin and feeling them absent-mindedly, trying to remember the rules of ripeness. Had he ever known how to tell a ready-to-eat avocado?

Probably not. He had people for that.

Suddenly he was aware of a presence near him. He looked up.

A six-foot-tall human heart — red, veiny, and pulsating, dripping with some viscous fluid — was lounging against the cantaloupe display, as casually as if it shopped there every day.

"Jesus Christ," Jack exclaimed.

"Oh, did I startle you?" the Heart asked in Jack's own voice, but sounding much younger to him. "Gee, Jack, I'm so sorry to bother you."

"What the fuck is going on?" Jack asked. He looked around as if to locate someone else and check if they could see this monstrosity. There was no one around.

"If you feel startled, imagine how I felt when you treated me like shit for about 40 years and then I stopped beating for 20 seconds," the

Heart said. "I thought it was over for me. How do you think that felt?"

Jack's first thought was that he must've taken too much of one of the dozens of pills his doctor had prescribed, and now he was hallucinating.

His second thought was that his Heart was kind of an asshole. If it really was his heart.

"Yes, you're imagining me," the Heart said, in answer to his unspoken question. "There isn't such a thing as a giant talking Heart."

Jack closed his eyes for a second and then opened them again. The Heart was still there. "You're not going to wish me away," the Heart said. "I have a message for you, and the message must get through."

"Awright,"Jack growled. "Just spit it out and then beat it."

The Heart appeared unfazed by Jack's award-winning growl. It settled back against the melons as if it were going to stay awhile.

"Not only have you not been taking care of your literal heart," the Heart said, "but you haven't been tending to your metaphoric heart either."

Jack scowled. "So I haven't had the best marriages," he said. "First one was a starter marriage. Everyone needs a starter marriage just to get to the real marriage. Second one was a gold digger. I think I'm still paying off the bitch. Third one was all right. I liked Diane. But she found someone else. That heart surgeon, or whatever the fuck kind of surgeon."

If an oversized organ could adopt a professorial demeanor, the Heart did so now. "I'm not just talking about legal contracts," it said. "I'm talking about opening up to people. Being vulnerable. Besides healthy eating and exercise, it's the best way to take care of me."

Jack's growl deepened to the extent that if a Fortune reporter had been there, they would have written a follow-up piece. "Vulnerable? Are you kidding me? You know how far that would get you in business? They can spot weakness from a mile away. Vulnerable, my ass!"

"I'm not talking about being weak," the Heart said patiently. "I'm talking about being flexible enough so you don't break. I'm talking about emotional awareness. I'm talking about becoming a man that women can stand to be around, so you can then find a woman willing to spend the last decades of your life with you."

"Decades?" Jack was still in growl mode. "Who says I have decades?"

"I do," the Heart said. "If you follow my advice. Maybe it's selfish, but I prefer to keep ticking. The point is," it continued, shifting its glistening bulk a fraction, "that being strong made you weak. You wouldn't have had a heart attack if you'd taken care of yourself."

Right then the two prostitutes walked into the produce section.

"Oh my God, look at that giant heart," one of them squealed and walked right up to the thing and poked it. The other rubbed its side with her hand. "It's so soft!"

The heart shimmied. "Hello, ladies," it said.

Jack stared at the women. "You two hookers can see this thing?"

"Hey, asshole!" one of the women yelled, pointing at him. "You do *not* use that word."

"Anyway," the other said, "We're not hookers, you slut-shaming douchebag. We just came from a club. This is what people wear in the present, while you're busy living in the past. The world will be a better place when all you old white men die off."

No one had talked that way to Jack in years. Speechless, he stared at the two women, trying to understand how they could dress that way and not expect to be confused with women of the night.

"I'm — sorry," he said, his voice tripping over the unaccustomed words. One of his rules was Never Apologize, but apparently this was a night for the unexpected. "I — didn't —"

"Yeah, well, fuck off," one of them threw over her shoulder as she gave the Heart a final pat and they drifted toward the exit.

Jack glared at the Heart. "You said I was imagining you," he said.

"Did I?" the Heart said airily. "It's so hard to remember with all the bullshit flying around here."

"The only bullshit is coming from you," Jack said. It made sense, though, that his heart would be a bullshitter. "I'm checking out," he said.

The Heart slapped along behind Jack as he motored to the solitary open checkout counter.

The homeless man shuffled up to the Heart as they passed. "Hey, buddy, you got any spare change? Every little helps."

"Nah, sorry," the Heart said. "I'm a selfish prick."

The homeless man giggled. "Fair enough."

The Heart waved its superior vena cava in Jack's direction. "Ask him, though," it said. "He's rich and carries a huge amount of cash."

Jack reluctantly dug out his wallet and forked over the first bill he found.

"A hundred dollars!" the homeless man marveled. "Thank you, sir. Thank you very much!"

"You're welcome," Jack growled. He looked at the Heart. "Happy now?"

The Heart waggled a pulmonary vein noncommittally. "It's a start," it said. "Use some of that ruthless ambition you claim to have and do better."

Jack set his loaf of bread and three avocados on the conveyor belt.

"What's a good-looking guy like you doing out this time of night?" the woman at the checkout counter asked, grabbing the first avocado.

"That doesn't make any sense," Jack said. "My looks do not determine my schedule."

"Feisty, too," the woman laughed. "I like it."

Jack stared at her. She was surprisingly attractive, and in his age range. He heard the Heart clear its throat behind him.

"Come to think of it," Jack said, hesitantly, since besides trying to apologize to the two scantily-clad young women, it had been quite awhile since he'd said anything nice, "What's a good-looking gal like you working the graveyard shift?"

"Can't sleep," the woman said, ringing up Jack's loaf of bread. "So I figured I might as well be working."

"Can't sleep, huh?" Jack said. "Me neither. At least at night. Say, when do you get off work? I'll buy you breakfast. Or as we insomniacs call it, dinner."

The cashier laughed. "Eight. You're on."

Jack felt his face smile and wondered what the fuck was going on. It felt strange. He could feel approval radiating from the Heart behind him, and the back of his neck burned with the annoyance of being condescended to.

Still, a date was a date.

"I'm Jack," he said. "My driver and I will pick you up. Big black Mercedes, license plate IOWNYOU."

"Oh, we're confident, are we?" the cashier said. "And fancy, too. Well, that suits me fine, Jack. I'm Meg. And you owe me nine dollars and eighty-three cents."

Jack handed her a hundred-dollar bill. "Keep the change," he said.

Meg stared at him. "That's not how grocery shopping works, honey."

Jack seized the bag of groceries and tossed it into the scooter basket in front of him. Then he laid on the throttle.

"What do I know?" he threw over his shoulder. "I'm just an idiot riding an electric wheelchair."

He heard Meg laughing behind him. He heard the Heart say, "Put this on his tab." He swiveled and saw the oversized organ ringing up a big bottle of aspirin.

"Come on," Jack growled at his scooter, willing it to go faster.

Tyler helped him into the back seat and then steered the car out of the parking lot.

A giant Heart lurched out of the store entrance with a bottle of pills tucked between its aortic arch and pulmonary trunk. It stood watching the Mercedes drive away.

"See you soon, Jack," it said.

THE GOOD ENOUGH AMERICAN NOVEL

"I'm having a terrible time with the plot," Jerome said. He was drinking a Hemingway daiquiri. He was not supposed to have grapefruit juice while taking a statin, but he really, really needed the daiquiri.

His ex-wife Chloe sat across from him at her outdoor patio table and sipped on her own daiquiri, the non-Hemingway variety.

Jerome and Chloe had moved on to other wives and husbands, but that didn't stop them from having an occasional drink together when their spouses were out of town.

"So which one is this? And where are you in it now?" Chloe asked.

"Oh God," Jerome groaned. "This is the one I told you about that I've tentatively titled *The Great American Novel*." He flipped open his laptop and squinted at the screen in the glare of the late-afternoon sun. "She's just realized who her mother was and that her husband, the barber, is hiding a secret, but that's not enough. I've written myself into a corner. It's like I don't know what happens next for her. The whole thing has gotten really unexciting for a thriller."

"You want to know what I think?" Chloe said suddenly, bouncing up in the metal chair and setting her drink on the table.

Jerome blinked. "Yes. That's why I'm complaining to you right now. In hopes that you'll have a great plot idea."

"This isn't a plot idea," Chloe said. "It's a theory about why writing a novel is difficult for you even though you're a natural at putting down words on paper."

Jerome sat back. "Hit me."

"You want everything in life to be smooth. Was it Stephen King who said 'kill your darlings'? You don't have the grit to kill your darlings.

You envelop your darlings in a cushion of front- and side-impact airbags. But what makes good reading is tension, crisis, and danger. Your writing reflects the way you want life to be, not the hero's journey of a good story."

Jerome thought about what she had said, trying not to be annoyed. She was always right, which had made parallel parking with her in the passenger seat especially irksome.

"You're right," he finally said. "I really have no ambition, which makes it hard to give it to my characters."

Chloe pointed two fingers at him and put an imaginary bullet between his eyes. "Exactly."

"Damn," Jerome said. "Maybe I should just give it up. I mean, ambition doesn't grow on trees. I must have gotten fucked up somehow during my formative years. My mother must not have breastfed me aggressively enough or something."

"I don't know," Chloe said and then tossed back the remainder of her drink with a flip of her wrist. "But it's clear that your writing is as milquetoast as you are."

"I don't think that's quite the right word," Jerome said. "But extra points for an impressive vocabulary. What do you suggest I do with the plot?"

"Go crazy!" Chloe said. "Do something nuts with your writing. Make your character do something out of character!" She tossed her daiquiri glass over her shoulder, where it hit the bike rack by the back door and shattered.

"Jesus, Chloe," Jerome said. "You didn't have to cover the patio with dangerous glass shards just to prove a point. You gotta remember where you are, which is not a bar in Puerto Vallarta."

"I had to do that," Chloe said, flaring her nostrils, "to demonstrate that courage can attack suddenly and take no prisoners. If you don't mix it up, you might as well call it *The Good Enough American Novel* because that's all it will ever be."

"Fine," Jerome said. He peered at his laptop screen. "Excuse me for a second. I'm going to write something right now and see what you think."

"Great," Chloe said. "I'm going to go and make us two more cocktails."

Jerome sat and stared at his laptop and then began to type. He barely registered Chloe coming back out, crunching across the broken glass and setting a drink down next to him.

She sat down across from him and then he heard her exclaim in a strangled way, "What the fuck? What's going on?"

Jerome looked up. Chloe was taller than she had been, and her hair had changed from brown to black. Now she was feeling around on the table, trying to find her drink.

"I can't see!" Chloe shrieked. "Something's happened to my eyes!"

"It's fine," Jerome said. "I've made you blind. You said I had trouble putting my protagonists in challenging situations."

"I can't feel my feet!" Chloe wailed.

Jerome cleared his throat. "I should say I also made you paralyzed from the waist down. That will give the barber an excuse to push you around in a wheelchair."

"He'll hate that!" Chloe screamed. "When Dylan gets back from the hair product convention in Dallas, he is so going to kick your ass!"

Jerome went back to typing. "This is great," he said. "I'm seeing new possibilities with the plot now that I've given my main character all these physical difficulties."

Chloe didn't say anything, as Jerome had just made her mute as well as blind. Then he shook his head. That didn't really work. He deleted the sentence.

"You FUCKER!" Chloe yelled.

Jerome reached across the table and squeezed her groping hand. "Thanks for the advice," he said. "You really are always right."

www.ingramcontent.com/pod-product-compliance
Lightning Source LLC
Chambersburg PA
CBHW061222210726
48294CB00006B/1944